DINO-MIKE

AND THE
LIVING FOSSILS

WRITTEN & ILLUSTRATED BY FRANCO

STONE ARCH BOOKS
a capstone imprint

Dino-Mike! is published by
Stone Arch Books,
a Capstone imprint
1710 Roe Crest Drive
North Mankato, Minnesota 56003
www.mycapstone.com

Cataloging-in-Publication Data is available on
the Library of Congress website.

ISBN: 978-1-4965-2489-8 (library hardcover)
ISBN: 978-1-4965-2493-5 (paperback)
ISBN: 978-1-4965-2497-3 (eBook)

Summary: Dino-Mike is on a dig in China when he
finds a mysterious dinosaur fossil that has four
wings. Mike celebrates his rare find — until the
party gets crashed by the gigantic P-Rex!

Printed in US.
102015   007538CGS16

CONTENTS

Young Mike Evans travels the world with his dino-hunting dad and his best friend, Shannon. From the Jurassic Coast in Great Britain to the Liaoning Province in China, young Dino-Mike has been there, *dug* that!

When his dad is dusting fossils, Mike's boning up on his own dino skills — only he's finding the real deal. A live T. rex egg! A portal to the Jurassic Period!! An undersea dinosaur sanctuary!!!

Prepare yourself for another wild and wacky Dino-Mike adventure, which nobody will ever believe . . .

Chapter 1

BORED IN CHINA

"Isn't this exciting?!" Mike's dad, Dr. Evans, asked.

Mike didn't think so. In fact, he was bored stiff. Standing in a giant pit digging up fossilized bones couldn't compare to facing off with living dinosaurs.

But Mike didn't want to disappoint his father. So he said, "Yeah! I never thought we'd be digging for dinosaur bones in China."

Mike and his father were working with a paleontological dig team. People with shovels and tiny brushes were everywhere.

"Not only are we in China," Dr. Evans said, "But we're hunting for the very rare Qianzhousarus Sinensis! A fearsome tyrannosaurus-class dinosaur!"

"The Pinocchio Rex," Mike said.

"Exactly!" his dad said. "Due to its particularly long snout. Mike, this could be the most important discovery of my career!"

Mike's father lived for the thrill of the chase. Well, the thrill of the search.

Dr. Evans could read the expression on his son's face. "Don't look so glum buddy. We'll find something here soon — I can feel it."

"I know," Mike said.

He couldn't tell his father why he was bored. His dad was chased dinosaur bones for a living, but Mike had actually been chased by dinosaurs — living ones!

It was hard to go back to playing with tiny shovels after that.

Dr. Evans gestured to the piles of dirt in front of them. "I think this is a complete set of Dinosaur bones! That's a rare find. Usually we have to recreate the missing bones as best we can for a museum." He spread his arms even wider. "But with this P-Rex, and the C. Yangi at the next site over, may be the world's first complete skeletons."

Mike smiled. "That's great, Dad."

Dr. Evans looked at his son. "I know, it's not the most exciting thing to you," Dad said. "But that'll change as soon as Shannon gets here."

"Shannon is coming?" Mike asked.

"Yep! I got a message from Dr. Broome that she's on her way."

"Weird," Mike said. "I just sent her some dig photos. She didn't mention anything about coming here."

"Dr. Broome mentioned those photos, actually," Dr. Evans said. "He took an interest in some feathers in your photo."

Mike pulled out his phone and scrolled through the pictures.

He found a photo he'd taken of a bunch of feathers near one of the dig sites. Mike didn't find anything super-interesting about it. A man like Dr. Broome was so smart that he probably recognized the feathers of some rare species worth investigating.

Dr. Broome spent most of his time in his underwater research complex. He sent his daughter on most excursions. The fact that Shannon was coming made Mike cheer up.

Moments later, a limousine pulled up to the edge of the dig site. The driver quickly exited the car and opened the back door.

Shannon bounced out from the back seat, her long red hair bobbing along with her.

Another familiar face emerged: Ms. Li Jing, their official guide. She was also their liaison — a fancy word that meant she communicated between Dr. Broome's research foundation and the Chinese government.

Then a third passenger emerged. The creature leapt out and bounced to Ms. Li Jing. Mike couldn't believe his eyes. Is that a Panda? he wondered.

Mike stared at the strange animal. He hadn't even noticed Shannon was standing right next to him.

"Well that's the worst 'Hello' I've ever gotten," said Shannon.

Mike snapped out of his trance. Instead of saying hi, he asked, "You rode here in a car with Panda?"

Dr. Evans laughed. "That's not a Panda," he said. "It's a dog."

Mike raised an eyebrow. "It's a fad here in China," Shannon explained. "They sometimes dye a pet's fur to make them look like exotic animals."

The panda-dog-thing jumped up on Shannon.

"My apologies Dr. Evans," said Ms. Li Jing. "I could not bear to leave my precious little Ahfu alone again."

I hope it will not be a bother."

Mike's dad leaned down and petted Ahfu. "Not a problem, Ms. Li Jing," he said. "I love dogs. If I didn't do so much traveling, I'd have one too."

That explains why he never let me have a dog, thought Mike.

"Would you like me to show you what we've found so far?" Dr. Evans asked.

"Yes, please," said Ms. Li Jing. She turned to Mike and Shannon. "Would you mind keeping an eye on Ahfu?"

"Sure!" said Mike. He patted his leg and said, "Ahfu, come on boy."

Apparently Ahfu understood English, because he loyally stood by Mike's side as they walked along the edge of the dig site. "I'm so glad you're here," Mike said to Shannon. "China is fascinating, but this dig is so dull! There's nothing but bones here!"

"Good thing you sent that picture of the feathers, then," she said.

Mike shrugged. "The one with a bunch of bird feathers? I was just bored and snapping photos of stuff."

Shannon smirked. "Mike . . . those feathers belong to a dinosaur!"

Chapter 2

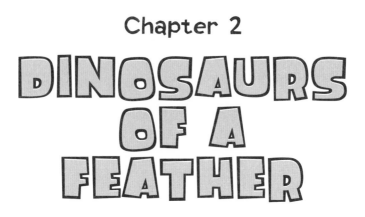

DINOSAURS OF A FEATHER

"A dinosaur?" Mike said. "But those feathers were still fresh, not fossilized. That means . . ."

Shannon grabbed his shoulders. "They came from a living dinosaur! Show me where you found them — now!" she said.

Mike nodded. "This way!"

The two of them jogged toward the nearby forest, Ahfu at their heels.

"Is this for real?" Mike asked as they ran. "Your dad's sure it's a living dino?"

"Yep!" Shannon said between breaths. "Dad said they belong to Changyuraptor Yangi, or C. Yangi for short."

Mike couldn't believe he was looking for a living dinosaur again.

"How does a dinosaur that's been extinct for — like, forever — show up in modern day China?" Mike asked.

"No idea," Shannon said. "But I'm here to find out!"

Mike huffed and puffed his way to the area where the feathers had been. He finally came to a stop beneath a particularly old, gnarled tree.

"The feathers were right here!" he
said, pointing to the ground. "I took the
picture just yesterday. Maybe the wind
swept them away?"

"Has it been windy lately?" asked
Shannon.

Mike flushed red. "No," he admitted, and changed the subject. "Okay, so what kind of dino are we looking for? And how did it get here?"

Shannon let a little smile slip across her lips. "What kind of dinosaur? Well that's easy: it's a C. Yangi. It's kind of like a gigantic turkey with a really long tail."

Mike felt relieved. Facing off with a giant turkey didn't sound so bad. "So not that big compared to some others we've come across?" he asked.

"Yes," said Shannon. "Though they are closely related to velociraptors and have the same nasty hooks on their hind wings."

Mike squinted. "Hind wings?"

"Oh!" said Shannon. "I guess I forgot to mention it. My bad. This is a four-winged micro-raptor."

Mike tilted his head. "Four wings? I think I would've noticed a giant turkey with four wings flying around here . . ."

Shannon shrugged. "Its tail is also twice as long as its body," she said. "The wings on its hind legs were probably used for slowing down its descent before swooping down to grab its prey."

Mike gulped. "Prey, huh . . ." While they talked and searched the surrounding tree line. Right then, Ahfu stopped and growled.

Shannon asked, "What is it, boy?"

Ahfu sniffed along the ground, growling the entire way. When Ahfu reached a particular tree, the fur on the back of its neck stood up. It leaned back a bit on its hind legs as if ready to pounce.

Shannon slowly inched her way up the tree. Then she reached up and pulled on one of its branches.

"Be careful," Mike said.

Shannon nodded at Mike's warning. The leaves began to rustle violently. Just then, a big ball of feathers came bursting out from the branches.

Mike heard himself yell, **"SHANNON, LOOK OUT!"**

Chapter 3

FLYING RAPTOR?!

Shannon ducked just in time as this feathered and freaky dinosaur buzzed past her head.

As it sprang from the tree and flew over their heads to another tree behind them, Mike couldn't help but admire the creature. After all, no one had seen the species alive for millions of years.

Most dinosaurs resembled lizards in one way or another, but this one looked like nothing he'd seen before.

Just like Shannon had described, it had raptor claws and four wings. But to Mike, it looked more like an eagle crossed with a lizard.

The C. Yangi lifted its tail with alarming speed. It was easily twice as long as the rest of its body.

As it settled on the branch, its eyes rested on Mike and Shannon. Ahfu, still nearby, barked at it.

"Quiet!" Mike yell-whispered to Ahfu. He turned to his friend. "What do we do now, Shannon?"

Shannon slowly pulled out a small black box from her pocket. Mike recognized it as one of her Dino traps.

"First we try to capture it," she whispered. "Then we try to find out how it got here."

Shannon fiddled with the controls. "When I get this back to my dad's lab, we can figure out where and when this dinosaur came from."

The C. Yangi turned its head slightly to watch Shannon.

Shannon cautiously approached the dinosaur with the trap.

Mike noticed that Ahfu had stopped barking. "Good dog," he whispered. But when he looked to his side, he saw Ahfu staring at another tree.

"Shannon!" Mike yell-whispered.
"The dog stopped barking!"

Shannon kept inching closer to the C.
Yangi. "So what?" she whispered

"It's just sitting there staring at a tree,"
Mike said. "What if there's another . . .
what if our feathered friend has a brother?

Shannon stopped and turned to look
at the dog. "Good point. You can never be
too careful when dealing with dinosaurs."

"Look!" said Shannon, pointing.

Mike saw a white object appear in
the middle of the forest. *Is that a floating
skull?!* he wondered.

Chapter 4

THE FLOATING SKULL

A strange whistling rang out. Despite the nervous feeling in his gut, Mike crept closer. He saw it wasn't a just a skull! A man's form stood amidst the leaves and shadows, camouflaged by them.

The whistling grew louder. *He's calling to the turkey-dino-thing!* Mike realized.

Mike pulled Shannon to the ground.

Just then, the C. Yangi swooped down from behind. Mike felt feathers graze the top of his head.

The strange dinosaur buzzed

right over them!

When Mike looked up, the C. Yangi was hovering in front of them. It held Shannon's dino tool in a claw, and crushed it like a stale cookie.

Mike rolled back to his feet, ready to protect his friend. Incredibly, the C. Yangi went directly to the mysterious skull-masked guy.

"Shannon — are you okay?" Mike asked, helping her to her feet.

Shannon nodded. When Mike looked back up, both the C. Yangi and the masked man were gone.

"Where did he go?" Mike asked.

Shannon rubbed her shin. "I'm not sure," she said.

Mike wracked his brain: they'd had trouble with dinosaurs before, and it always stemmed from people associated with the same place: Atlantis, Shannon's underwater family home and dinosaur research center.

Shannon interrupted Mike's thoughts. "Hey, Ahfu is gone!"

Mike darted around trees, looking for the panda-like pooch. "Do you think he chased after them?" Mike asked.

"If he was chasing them, we'd still hear him barking," Shannon said.

Mike gasped. "Do you think they dognapped Ahfu?!"

"Not likely," Shannon said.

"We would've heard barking or a struggle." Shannon said. "Ahfu probably just got scared and went back to Ms. Li Jing at Base Camp."

Mike gasped. "What if this turkey-dino tool-crusher is headed there?!"

As one, they sprinted toward the camp. "What do we do if it's already there?" Mike asked.

"I don't have any more traps," she said. "But We'll figure something out."

They arrived at the dig site out of breath and panicked, but everything seemed fine. No dinosaurs. Everyone was still working. No sign of the masked man. No strange whistling to be heard.

Shannon pointed "Mike, look!"

He saw it before she'd even spoke: Ahfu was happily weaving in and out between Mike's dad's legs.

"Good, Ahfu's safe," Mike said. "Ms. Ling should make him look like a chicken for running away like that."

They joined Ms. Li Jing and Dr. Evans. "I'm so sorry," she said. "That phone call took longer than I expected."

"No worries," Dr. Evans said happily.

Ms. Li Jing turned to Mike and Shannon. "I appreciate the two of you taking Ahfu for a walk. Out of curiosity, where did you go?"

"Um," Mike said. He wasn't sure what to say due to the dinosaur, adrenaline rush, masked man, and the ensuing sprint. "We saw some weird thing —"

Shannon interrupted him. "And we weren't quite sure what it was, so we figured it'd be safer here at the site."

Shannon was probably right to lie. Mike had a hard time believing his dad would buy their story. Heck, Mike had a hard time believing it himself.

"The dinosaur is gone!" said Arthur, Dr. Evan's assistant.

"What?!" asked Dr. Evans.

"We were about to start excavating in the new quadrant," Arthur said.

Arthur took a deep breath. "My team and I headed over there," he said. "The entire fossil is just . . . gone. *Vanished*."

Together, the group scurried over to the C. Yangi dig site. The cordoned off area had no fossils. Instead, there was a perfect skeletal impression in the dirt.

"See?" Arthur cried. "It's gone!"

"But how?" Dr. Evans asked. "How could someone have done this without us knowing about it? And so quickly!"

Shannon pulled Mike to the side. "You don't think that's the same C. Yangi that we just saw, do you?" she asked.

"That's crazy!" Mike whispered. "The C. Yangi we saw was flying around!"

"Crazy?" Shannon said. "After time traveling and bringing real dinosaurs to the present, you think *this* is crazy?"

Mike had to admit she had a point. Her dad's technology could do just that. "Do you think anyone else has the same technology as your father?"

"Doubtful," Shannon said. "My dad is the only one that knows how to time-travel. Besides, why reanimate fossilized bones when you can just zap back in time to get them?"

Before Mike could answer, they overheard Ms. Li Jing say, "Perhaps this is the work of *Mr. Bones*."

The creepy dude from the forest! Mike thought.

Chapter 5

RISE OF THE P-REX!

Shannon spoke before Mike could. "Who is Mr. Bones?" she asked.

"More like a what than a who," said Ms. Li Jing. "It's a local legend."

Dr. Evans laughed. "I'm sure she's just pulling your leg, kids."

Ms. Li Jing smirked. "They are just folklore," she said. "However, there is a local legend of a farmer who haunts the countryside for those who wronged him in life."

Mike narrowed his eyes. "Ghost?"

Ms. Li Jing smiled. "Like I said —
they're just stories."

*The skull-faced dude looked real
enough,* Mike thought.

Dr. Evans sighed. "Well, we better take
a look around and see what we can find."

"Good idea," said Ms. Li Jing. "I will
head back to my car to call my superiors
to let them know what has happened
here." She headed back to the other dig
site. Ahfu trotted by her side.

"You two better head back that way
too," Dr. Evans said. "This is crime scene
now, so I want to keep the site from
getting trampled."

Arthur interrupted. "Dr. Evans, we found a strange powdery substance we would like you to examine."

"I'll be right there," Dr. Evans said. "Mike, I want you two to go back to my trailer and wait for me to return."

Mike's dad walked off. "Let's go," Shannon said to Mike. "I'll call my dad. Maybe he can help."

They walked along the solitary path through the woods. Shannon asked, "You don't think it's a real ghost, right?"

Mike shrugged. "Nah. Looked like some dude wearing a mask."

When they reached the main site, Mike stopped. "Mike?" Shannon said.

Mike was staring up at the sky. He opened his mouth but didn't speak.

Sharon followed Mike's gaze. Her eyes went wide. "The Pinocchio Rex!" she said.

The P-Rex had noticed them, too. They stared at each other, then the P-Rex reared back. Shannon braced herself for what was going to be the loudest thing they'd hear that day. But when the P-Rex opened its mouth and the muscles on its neck vibrated . . . but no sound came out.

Shannon noticed the green halo surrounding the P-Rex's head. "Look!" she said, pointing a finger. "The floating skull!"

The man in the mask was holding a device that emitted green light. The light extended to the head of the dinosaur and surrounded it like a bubble.

Before Mike could figure out why it was silent, the P-Rex's giant jaws snapped shut just a few inches in front of him. Its jaws hadn't made a sound.

Shannon pulled Mike back in case the P-Rex attacked again. Before Mike could speak, Shannon was on the move.

"You distract the dinosaur," Shannon said. "I'll see what Mr. skeleton-face is up to!"

She was into the woods and out of sight before Mike could say, "Wait — what?!"

Mike scrambled backward as the P-Rex snapped at him again. The eerie silence remained.

Mike ran behind a tree to try to confuse the dinosaur, but the P-Rex just shattered the tree in half with its jaws — silently!

The device Mr. Bones has must be canceling sound waves, Mike guessed. *Like dad's noise canceling headphones, or something.*

Mike turned and ran toward Mr. Bones to see if he could get the P-Rex to turn around. Mike could see Mr. Bones clearly. He was dressed in an all black suit, overcoat, shirt, and tie.

His black mask was more like a hood that completely covered his head. It had a white skull emblazoned on the front.

Mike pulled up his hood. Just as he was about to activate his dino jacket's super-speakers, Shannon leaped out of the woods from a tree branch.

WHAM! She smashed into Mr. Bones!

The device he was holding fell from his hand as he hit the ground. The green halo surrounding the head of the P-Rex disappeared.

The P-Rex's roar that made Mike's ears ring. The sound was so close that he knew it was close behind. *Too* close.

Mr. Bones scrambled to his feet.

"Mike, grab him!" yelled Shannon.

Mike rolled away from the P-Rex's jaws. "Little busy here!" he yelled.

Shannon grunted. "Why do they always chase after you?" she asked.

"Sheer luck!" Mike said sarcastically, doing his best to avoid getting eaten.

Shannon raced at Mr. Bones.

Mr. Bones pulled something from his pocket and pointed it at Shannon.

Mike yelled, "Shannon, look out!"

Then Mr. bones turned the device toward the P-Rex. **CLICK!**

A rush of air blasted by Mike. It felt like he'd been caught in a vacuum.

The P-Rex began to wobble and distort like a flag whipping in the wind.

POP! Just like that, P-Rex was gone. Sprinkles of white dust floated to the ground where the dinosaur had been.

"Did you just disintegrate that dinosaur?" Shannon asked Mr. Bones.

The figure stayed silent. Instead, he pointed the device at himself.

POP! The same sudden rush of air and sound followed. He had vanished in a cloud of white dust.

Mike raised an eyebrow. "What the heck just happened?"

Shannon shrugged. "No idea."

Dr. Evans and Arthur emerged from the trees behind them. "Mike, is that you?" Dr. Evans asked.

"Um . . . yeah, Dad. We're over here."

"What in the world was that roar we just heard?" Dad asked.

Mike's eyes rolled up and to the right. "Um," was all he could think to say.

"The roar came from Mike," said Shannon. "His dino jacket's speakers."

"Yeah!" Mike said, following her lead. "She asked to hear them. I just had the volume up too high. Sorry."

Dr. Evans glanced around, his eyes wide. "What happened here?" he cried. "The dig site is completely ruined!"

Uh-oh, thought Mike. *That P-Rex stomped all over it. No way I'm gonna be able to explain my way outta this.*

Dr. Evans bent down to examine the dig area. "The P-Rex bones! They're all gone!" he said. "Even the ones we hadn't dug up yet!"

Dr. Evans cradled his face in his hands. "How could this happen? Who could have done this?"

On the other side of the site, Arthur was helping Ms. Li Jing to her feet near some bushes. She was wiping her forehead and pulling twigs and leaves from her hair.

"I saw who it was," Ms. Li Jing said, leaning wearily on Ahfu. "It was Mr. Bones!"

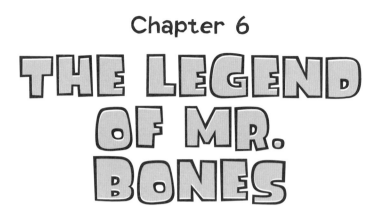

Chapter 6

THE LEGEND OF MR. BONES

Arthur helped Ms. Li Jing to her feet. "She was passed out in the bushes over there," he explained.

"It was terrifying!" said Ms. Li Jing.

"What did you see?" asked Dr. Evans.

"All I saw was a skull," she said quietly. "A floating skull. I'm ashamed to say that I fainted at the sight of it."

Dr. Evans looked around. "Did anyone else see anything?"

Everyone shook their heads. "Well, whatever it was," Dr. Evans said, "Mike must've scared it away with that T. rex roar from your sweatshirt."

"Um, yeah," said Mike. "Must have."

"Is this skull guy real?" asked Arthur.

"I don't know," said Dr. Evans. "As a paleontologist, I believe in cold, hard facts." He turned to look at the missing bones in the dig site. "The facts are: the bones were stolen right out from under us, and I have no idea how. But I *do* know that this place isn't safe."

He turned to Mike and Shannon, "I'm going to stay here and help pack up, but you two are leaving immediately."

"But, Dad —" Mike started.

"No arguments, Mike," Dad said. "I'm not putting you or Shannon in any more danger here."

Shannon spoke up before Mike could. "Of course, Dr. Evans. We'll head back to my dad's lab. It's safe there."

Dr. Evans smiled at Shannon and nodded at her.

"Why did you say that?" Mike whispered.

"Look, if we want to find out what happened here, I think it's better if we're investigating things on our own," Shannon said. "We don't want your dad — or anyone else — to get hurt, right?"

"Yeah, I suppose," Mike said. "We better find this Mr. Bones character before anyone else does."

Then they heard Ms. Li Jing say, "Of course, Dr. Evans. I will take these two to the city and get them on the first plane out."

"Thank you," Dad said. "It's a huge relief knowing they'll be safe with you."

Mike and Dr. Evans hugged each other goodbye. Ms. Li Jing was already inside her car with Ahfu, his nose pressed against the glass. The driver, sweating in his suit, held the door open for Mike and Shannon. The two friends climbed inside.

Mike watched as the site grew smaller as they drove away. The ride was quiet for a while. Except for Ahfu, who seemed happy to more people along for the ride.

"So . . . you didn't get a good look at him?" Shannon asked Ms. Li Jing. "Mr. Bones, I mean."

Ms. Li Jing spoke. "I did not see much of anything. The whole thing was much too frightening. I do not believe in myths, but I definitely saw *something*."

Mike looked out the window and sighed. He wanted to solve this mystery. "I hope my dad's okay," he said.

Ms. Li Jing smiled.

"Do not be alarmed, Michael," she said. "I'm sure Dr. Evans has everything under control. We will arrive at the airport soon. Why don't you have something to drink? There is some water in a cooler in the front seat."

Mike suddenly realized how thirsty he was. "I'll take one of those," he said.

Mike bent over the back of his seat and opened the cooler. The driver, Chen, watched him as he reached inside. The water was buried in ice, so he reached out a little farther to grab it.

As he leaned in closer, he noticed something strange on the floor mats: sprinkles of white-gray powder.

Mike froze. The driver narrowed his eyes, so Mike smiled at the man. The driver politely nodded and refocused on the road.

Mike quickly back down in his seat. The driver was eyeing him suspiciously, so Mike went stone faced and stared straight ahead.

"What's the matter with you?" asked Shannon. "I thought you were getting a bottle of water."

"I'm . . . not thirsty," he said.

Everything in the car seemed unnaturally quiet. No one spoke. Even Ahfu was content sleeping by Ms. Li Jing's side.

Whenever Ms. Li Jing glanced at Mike,
he put on a big, fake smile. He had to alert
Shannon somehow. He thought of using
his phone, but it'd be obvious he was
texting Shannon when her phone went off.

I have to get them to stop the car somehow, he thought.

Mike held his stomach and groaned loudly enough to get everyone's attention. Even Ahfu lifted his head.

"Are you all right?" asked Shannon.

"No," Mike said weakly.

"What is wrong?" asked Ms. Li Jing.

Mike faked a burp. "Well . . . Arthur made chili last night. Now I feel like velociraptors are eating me from the inside."

Ms. Li Jing looked at him quizzically. "You have a dinosaur in your stomach?" she asked. "I do not understand."

Shannon smiled. "He means he needs to use the restroom," she said.

"Oh." She said. Then her eyes went wide. "OH! I see! We will be in the next village soon. We can stop there."

Mike doubled over. "I'm not sure I can make it," he said.

Ms. Li Jing called out to the driver. "Chen, please stop! Immediately! I do not want vomit in my limousine!"

As soon as the car stopped, Mike scrambled out. Shannon remained in the car, awkwardly smiling at Ms. Li Jing.

Mike came back a second later. He grabbed Shannon by the arm, and said, "I need you to stand guard for me!"

He dragged her out of the car. Ahfu excitedly exited as well, thinking it was playtime.

Mike led Shannon to the edge of the trees, then he went into the woods to pretend to poop.

"I don't see why I have to be with you out here," Shannon said, keeping her back to Mike. "Nobody's around."

Just loud enough for Shannon to hear, Mike said. "I don't have to go."

"What?" she said, spinning to look at him.

"Don't turn around!" he said from behind a tree. "I just needed to talk to you about Mr. Bones . . ."

"You could have talked to me in the car!" she said.

"Actually," Mike said, "I think Mr. Bones is *in the car*!"

"Ms. Li Jing?!" cried Shannon.

"No!" Mike whisper-yelled at her. "And keep your voice down."

Ms. Li Jing poked her head out the car's window. "Did you say my name?"

"Uh, no! He said he's almost done!" Shannon shouted back. Then she said to Mike, "What are you talking about?"

"The driver," said Mike.

67

"The guy is dressed in a black suit, and there's that white powdery substance all over the floor mats in the front seat," Mike said. "It's the same powder they found at the C. Yangi site. And it's the same stuff we saw floating around when the P-Rex disappeared!"

Ahfu was sniffing the ground around them. "What are we going to do?" Shannon asked.

Before Mike could answer, a familiar sound rang out. *POP*!

"Oh, no!" said Shannon. "The last time we heard that was . . ."

ROOOOAARRR! The giant P-Rex came running toward them.

No green bubble was around its head. Mike was thankful for that, at least. Mike grabbed Shannon and ran.

Mike heard barking. He turned back to see Ahfu standing his ground against the oncoming dino-beast.

Maybe he's not a chicken-dog after all, Mike thought. *Definitely dumb, though.*

Mike couldn't just let dog die, though. He grit his teeth, reached up, and pulled his dino hood over his head . . .

The giant P-Rex burst through the trees! Mike had mere seconds to save Ahfu.

He flipped a hidden switch in his jacket. The T. rex-like eyes on the hood of the jacket lit up, bathing everything around in white light. The loud and terrifying sound of a Tyrannosaurus rex emanated from his super-speakers, too.

The huge P-Rex came to a sliding stop, then immediately began to scramble away. Mike decided to press the advantage and run toward the P-Rex.

"It's working!" Mike cried.

The P-Rex stumbled out of the forest and onto the road . . . near the car!

Mike stopped and yanked off his hood. The lights and sounds ended.

Shannon came up behind him, panting from the sprint. "Why are you stopping?" she asked.

"He's too close to the —"

Mike was interrupted by the loud sound of crunching metal. The P-Rex had stumbled into the black vehicle.

"Oh, no!" cried Shannon. "Ms. Li Jing and Chen!"

Mike flipped his jacket's hood up and charged at the P-Rex. The startled dino scrambled away into the nearby forested area.

Mike ran to the car, afraid of what he might find inside. With great surprise, he saw that no one was in the car!

"That proves it!" Mike said. "Chen is Mr. Bones!"

"And now he has Ms. Li Jing!" added Shannon.

Mike heard Ahfu begin barking again. For some reason, it reminded him of the first time he heard Ahfu bark . . .

Mike yelled, "Look out!"

He pulled Shannon down next to the car just as the rush of air and the rustle of feathers swooped over their heads.

"The C. Yangi!" Mike said.

"It's back?" said Shannon "It's like an evil trained parrot, or something."

Mike rubbed his chin. "Like . . . Mr. Bones's pet?"

"Yes! That's exactly right!" came an unfamiliar voice. It was low and rumbling, like how a dinosaur chewing rocks might sound.

"We're not afraid of you!" Mike shouted at Mr. Bones.

"Then you truly are a foolish young man!" Mr. Bones said.

Smoke started to billow out from under his jacket. It looked like he was riding on it.

Shannon gasped. "Is he . . . floating?"

Mr. Bones moved his hand to his mouth. A whistling sound rang out, and the C. Yangi swooped back toward Mike and Shannon for another attack. Mike knew they wouldn't both be able to get out of the way, so he quickly unzipped his jacket and he wrapped it around himself and Shannon.

BEEP-BEEP-BEEP! The jacket inflated to the size of a small hot air balloon just as the C. Yangi hit them at full force!

The C. Yangi bounced off Mike and
Shannon like a trampoline. They went
flying away in opposite directions.

"Close call!" Shannon said.

Mike frowned and pointed toward
the forest. "We're not out of the woods
yet!" he warned.

ROAR! The P-Rex emerged from the tree line and charged at the balloon.

Mike sighed. "This is gonna hurt," he said, pinching his eyes shut.

BONK! Mike and Shannon bounced off the head of the P-Rex, ricocheted off is head, and smacked into Mr. Bones!

KA-POW! They knocked Mr. Bones off his column of smoke.

Mike and Shannon bounced a few times before coming to a stop. The jacket sensed they'd stopped moving, and deflated itself.

Mike let go of Shannon. They both scrambled back to their feet.

Ms. Li Jing was trapped inside a nearby green bubble surrounded by smoke. She yelled and banged her fist on the walls, but no sound came out. It reminded Mike of the containment field used in Dr. Broome's research lab.

Suddenly, the C. Yangi and the P-Rex came at them again.

When Mr. Bones held up his right hand, they both immediately stopped. "If you give up now, no harm will come to you!" Mr. Bones growled.

"We were right — he *can* control the dinosaurs!" said Shannon. "My father had been working on something similar to this, but could never get it to work."

Mike and Shannon ran for the trees. As they disappeared into the tree line, Mike heard the dinosaurs coming. "We can't leave Ms. Li Jing back there," Shannon said.

"Don't worry, we're not going to!" Mike said. "When you mentioned your dad, it gave me an idea."

They darted behind trees and changed directions as often as possible.

"In all the excitement, I forgot that your dad put a portal key my jacket!" Mike said. "If we can get to Ms. Li Jing, we can port out of this time to safety."

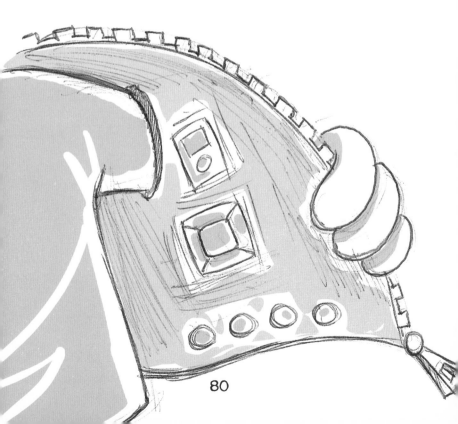

"Good idea!" said Shannon. "But we have to get away from the C. Yangi and the P-Rex first."

They continued running in a wide arc to make their way back to the car.

As they ran, Shannon said, "If he's bringing dinosaurs back to life, then he needs them whole. Complete skeletons!"

"So if there are any missing bones, then Mr. Bones wouldn't be able to reanimate them!" added Mike.

"Exactly!" Shannon said between breaths. "That must be why he's here at your dad's dig site! He knew they were going to dig up two intact dinosaur skeletons."

"I'm glad you're here," Mike said, panting. "Otherwise I'd be dino-chow by now."

Shannon blushed. "Nice moves back there with the balloon trick, by the way," she said. "You saved us both . . ."

Mike blushed. Shannon changed the subject.

"In any case," Shannon said, "now Chen is in control of two deadly dinos!"

Mike clenched his fist. "And we're the only ones who can stop him!"

Chapter 7

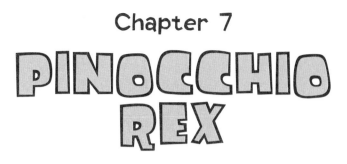
PINOCCHIO REX

Mike and Shannon managed to circle around to a better vantage point. Otherwise, the P-Rex would quickly find them soon due to its great sense of smell.

The C. Yangi would struggle to spot them due to the tree cover, as well. But they were anything but well-hidden.

From where they were, they could see the mangled car by the road.

Mr. Bones was pacing beside it in agitation. He seemed to be talking to his captive, Ms. Li Jing. As he spoke, he moved his right hand back and forth, opening and closing his fingers.

At the same time, the P-Rex was bounding up and down the side of the road, trying to sniff out Shannon and Mike. The C. Yangi was swooping from tree to tree in search of them as well.

"See?" said Shannon. "He's controlling them with his right hand! I bet he reanimated the C. Yangi first to make sure his tech worked. Then he lured us all away from the P-Rex dig site so he could reanimate him."

"You're probably right, as usual," said Mike. "Which means Mr. Bones could build himself a whole dinosaur army if he wanted to!"

Mike looked up to see the C. Yangi passing over them. "It's getting closer!" he said. "We have to move."

Mike and Shannon ran into the street just as the C. Yangi landed on the spot they had just been.

Both Mr. Bones and the P-Rex turned to look at them. Mr. Bones motioned with his hand, and the P-Rex stomped toward them. Mike moved away from Shannon and yelled in an attempt to have the P-Rex come after him instead.

Sure enough, the P-Rex turned and headed straight for Mike. "It worked!" he said, equally happy and terrified.

The P-Rex was only a few yards away from Mike when he heard the familiar sound of wings behind him. He turned to spot the C. Yangi swooping down rapidly from behind.

"Mike, you're surrounded!" Shannon yelled. Mike turned to see that Mr. Bones had caught up to Shannon and was holding her by the arm.

Mike looked back and forth from the C. Yangi, the charging P-Rex, and the skeletal grin of Mr. Bones. He didn't know what to do.

"Use the portal key!" Shannon yelled.

That would work, Mike thought quickly. *But Shannon would still be the hands of Mr. Bones . . .*

As the two dinosaurs closed in on him, he knew he had no choice. He mouthed the words, "I'll be back!" at Shannon.

Then he reached inside his jacket and flipped a switch.

Mike vanished.

Chapter 8

LOST IN TIME

Mike wasn't sure exactly where he was. All he knew for sure is that it was warm — and he was surrounded by dinosaurs.

He paced the rocky cliff overlooking the grassy plains. Herds of brachiosaurs below reached their long necks into the air. They reminded Mike of living construction cranes.

Under different circumstances, Mike would have marveled at them for hours. But right now, all he did was check the clock on his phone.

Time travel wasn't new to him. The glowing, protective aura around him was a result of the portal key. It would last until the key recharged, and Mike was sent back to present time.

Until then, all Mike could do was wait. He hated the fact that he'd had to leave Shannon in the hands of that crazy Mr. Bones, but he didn't know what else he could've done.

All the same, he felt terrible.

Mike checked the portal key.

The key was only about halfway recharged. He checked the clock on his cell phone. He'd been gone twenty-six minutes.

Each minute had felt like an hour. He tried to use the time to think of a plan to stop Mr. Bones, but he kept getting distracted. He was worried about Shannon.

Mike checked the charger again.

The key's energy was almost refilled. "So much for a plan," Mike said. "Guess I'll have to think on my feet . . ."

With that, he hit the **RETURN** button on the portal key. Once again, energy crackled around him. He started to glow, followed by a weird sensation of falling that he was sure he'd never get used to.

WHUMP! Mike landed on the road next to the mangled car in China. He frantically looked around, expecting the dinosaurs — or Mr. Bones — to attack him.

Mike saw nothing. He did, however, hear many birds chirping in the trees around him.

"If a large predatory animal like a P-Rex was around," Mike reasoned, "then the birds would be silent."

In the fifty-two minutes he'd been gone, Mr. Bones had escaped. That meant Shannon and Ms. Li Jing were with him — and in serious trouble.

Mike looked around for any indication of where they'd gone. The mangled car was still by the side of the road, so they'd had to travel on foot.

"Wait a second," Mike said. He bent at the waist and examined the road. A bunch of gravel looked different than before. It stretched along the area, as if it had been dug up.

Mike climbed on top of the smashed car to get a better look. For a second, he thought he could make out a letter 'R' scratched into the road.

"Weird," Mike muttered. "I need to get a better look at that."

Mike reached into his jacket and pushed the inflation mode button. **BEEP-BEEP-BEEP!** His jacket ballooned up like it had before.

Slowly, Mike lifted into the air positioned himself to look down on the road. "It's a message!" Mike realized. "That crazy Mr. Bones made the P-Rex scratch a note into the road with its huge talons."

A crudely drawn skull was traced next to the message.

That P-Rex is a pretty good artist for a dinosaur, thought Mike.

Mike looked for the sign of their location. Then he saw it: an abandoned warehouse nestled into the woods about a mile out from the road.

The metal building had trees and plants growing around it. It seemed to Mike that the trees were trying to swallow it up.

That's where they are, he thought. And now that he's seen some of the things my jacket can do, he wants it for himself.

That meant Mr. Bones was holding Shannon and Ms. Li Jing (and likely Ahfu) hostage. And he had two mind-controlled dinosaurs guarding them.

It was obviously a trap, but Mike didn't care. He clenched his fist. "It's time to finish this!"

Chapter 9

SHOWDOWN!

Mike stomped through the wide-open entrance to the abandoned warehouse. This was it. The big showdown. The final fight.

Mr. Bones had Shannon and Ms. Li Jing trapped in separate green containment fields.

"You can have them back," came Mr. Bones's gravelly voice. "If you give me your dino jacket!"

Mike saw the words Shannon mouthed the words, "Don't do it, Mike!"

She was right. As usual. The portal key alone would let Mr. Bones travel back in time. He'd have his own army of dinosaurs.

The idea of hundreds of dinosaurs roaming around the world at Mr. Bones's command made Mike shiver. He'd faced bad dudes before, but Mr. Bones was bad to the *bone*. A true super-villain.

Mike squinted into the darkness behind Shannon. He vaguely saw the outline of the P-Rex. The C. Yangi was easier to spot due to its bright purple feathers.

Hovering between the two dinos was the seemingly floating skull mask of Mr. Bones. His black suit was nearly invisible in the dark warehouse.

"Well, Dino-Mike?" Mr. Bones growled. "What's your answer — the jacket, or the lives of your friends?!"

Mike looked down at his jacket. He had to save Shannon and Ms. Li Jing, but giving up his jacket could mean the end of the world . . .

Mike raised his head. He stared at Mr. Bones. "Why do you want my jacket?" he asked.

Mr. Bones was silent. Mike's eyes were getting used to the low light.

Mike could see Mr. Bones' silhouette now. The creep was standing with his hand stretched out. "Give. Your. Jacket. To. Me!" he growled.

Mike looked at Shannon. She repeatedly mouthed the word: *No!*

Mike clenched his teeth. He unzipped his sweatshirt. But instead of taking it off, he yelled out, "NO WAY!!"

Mike's response reverberated through the cavernous building. Mr. Bones slowly closed his open fingers. A strange green light grew out from his clenched fist.

In seconds, the entire warehouse was illuminated in sickly green light. Mike clearly saw the P-Rex and C. Yangi.

A furious **RRRROOOARRRR!** sent shivers down Mike's spine. Mr. Bones ran different fingers over the green light in his palm, creating the same whistling noise from before.

The P-Rex stepped around Mr. Bones and dashed for Mike. As it got closer, the P-Rex lowered its mouth and opened its jaw, revealing every last one of its razor-sharp teeth.

Mike's entire body screamed at him to **RUN!** But Mike stood his ground and tried to judge the angle of the jaws as the P-Rex got closer and closer.

When the P-Rex was a foot away from him, Mike leapt onto its snout!

"Sorry about this!" Mike said. He
shoved his arms into the P-Rex's nostrils!

FWOOOOSH! A mint-green mist ejected from Mike's sleeves. The P-Rex snarled angrily, but he couldn't throw Mike off his face because Mike's arms were jammed in its nostrils.

Mike yanked his arms free and leapt off. When he hit the floor, he saw his hands were covered in dino-snot. "Ewwww," he said.

The P-Rex turned its head, opened it's jaws, and . . . **ACHOOOO!**

Mike was amazed — he'd never seen a dinosaur sneeze before! He looked over to see that Mr. Bones was now plastered to the wall with sticky dino-mucus!

The P-Rex shook its head to clear the cobwebs, and then lurched toward Mike!

Please work! Mike silently wished. *Please . . . work!*

The P-Rex loomed over Mike, its angry eyes bearing down on him, and opened its massive mouth. Mike lowered himself to the ground.

Why isn't it working?! he thought.

Just as the dinosaur's jaws were about to devour Mike, the P-Rex's eyes rolled back in their sockets. The giant beast began to sway from side to side.

Mike sprinted away, knowing what was about to happen.

WHUMP!!!

Mike cheered. "Dino down!" he cried.
Dr. Broome's knockout gas had taken a
little longer to work than he'd hoped.

Mike turned and glared at Mr. Bones.
The super-villain was still stunned and
stuck to the wall in dino snot. Either
that, or he was just too grossed out
to move.

Mike ran over to Shannon and Ms. Li Jing. He needed to free them before Mr. Bones regained his senses. Near Shannon's feet, he found a switch.

POP! He flipped it. Shannon's bubble disappeared.

"I can't believe you did that!" she said immediately. She wrapped her arms around Mike and squeezed him half to death. "Do you know how dangerous that was? You came this close to being gobbled up by that P-Rex!

Mike blushed and hugged her back.

"You fool!" Mr. Bones growled. He was one his feet now — flicking dino-boogers off his arms.

Mike positioned himself between Shannon and Mr. Bones. He reminded himself this wasn't over yet — he still needed to stop the super-villain — and save Ms. Li Jing.

Mr. Bones stared at the sleeping dinosaur. "What did you do to my poor P-Rex?" he cried.

Mike slowly moved toward Ms. Li Jing while Mr. Bones was distracted. "Knockout gas," he said, trying to keep the creep distracted. "Don't worry. The P-Rex will be just fine in a few hours."

If he could free Ms. Li Jing, he could probably get all three of them to safety. He could deal with Mr. Bones later.

Mike heard a familiar fluttering behind him. *The C. Yangi!* he realized.

Mr. Bones turned his attention back to Mike. Mike froze in his tracks. "That was a clever trick, I admit." Mr. Bones lowered his head. "You seem to have quite a lot of tricks up those sleeves of yours. But what I'm most interested in is the portal key . . ."

Mike narrowed his eyes. "How did you know about that?" he asked.

Mr. Bones came face to face with Mike. "You disappeared right in front of us," he growled. "You left these damsels in distress behind. I made your friend here tell me all about your precious key."

Shannon glared at Mr. Bones. "I'll show you damsel!" she yelled. To Mike, she added, "I had to tell him. He said he'd make the P-Rex crush Ms. Li Jing."

"Don't worry about it," said Mike. He turned to Mr. Bones. "What do you plan to do with it if I give it to you?"

Mr. Bones crossed his arms. "Take a wild guess," he said.

"You'll use the key to go back in time and reanimate more dinosaurs," Mike said. "Then you'll use that brainwashing thingy you have to control them."

Mr. Bones clapped lazily. "Very impressive," he said sarcastically. "You figured it out all about by yourself."

Mike turned to Shannon. "Your brother Jeff's plan was better," he said.

Shannon nodded. "Yeah. And guess what? Jeff didn't get away with it . . . and neither will this bag of bones!"

To Mike's wide-eyed surprised, Shannon charged right at Mr. Bones!

Mr. Bones tilted his head at Shannon. He quickly gestured with his right hand. Mike saw the C. Yangi swooping in from behind Shannon.

Shannon briefly turned to Mike — and winked at him.

Mike smiled. He knew exactly what his best friend was thinking . . .

Quickly, Mike pulled up his hood. He flipped all the switches for all of his super-special dino-jacket powers.

FWOOSH! FWOOSH! ROARRR!

As Mike expected, Mr. Bones raised his hands to shield his eyes from the blinding light coming from Mike's jacket.

Mr. Bones' erratic hand movement sent the C. Yangi flying up and away from Shannon.

Mike let out a little "Yes!"

Shannon's plan, however, wasn't complete. She reached Mr. Bones and wrapped her arms around his feet. She was too small to knock him over, but he was stuck in place.

"Now, Mike!" Shannon yelled.

Mike ran as fast as he could at Mr. Bones. When he had nearly reached him, he pushed a button inside his jacket.

FWOOSH! It inflated at the exact instant Mike smashed into Mr. Bones.

BOING!

The super-villain went flying from the impact — and disappeared into the shadows.

Mike quickly deflated. He and Shannon ran to Ms. Li Jing's bubble. Working together, they shut off the containment field and set Ms. Li Jing and Ahfu free.

"C'mon, let's get out of here!"
said Shannon.

Shannon headed for the entrance.
Ms. Li Jing limped along after her.

"Wait," Mike said, stopping them.
"We can't leave yet."

Shannon shook her head. "But —"

"Shannon, we have to take the P-Rex
with us," Mike said. "We can't leave
it here for Mr. Bones."Ahfu started
growling at the air above them. "And we
don't have much time."

Shannon frowned. "You're right,"
Shannon said. They ran toward the
unconscious P-Rex while Ahfu continued
barking at the air above them.

As they reached the P-Rex, Shannon turned to see Ms. Li Jing was still a good thirty feet behind them. "Hurry!" shouted Shannon. "Wait . . .why are you limping? Did you get injured?"

"I must have — twisted it," Ms. Li Jing said between gasps.

Ahfu's barking intensified as he joined the group. Mike was standing on top of the P-Rex, holding out his hand to Shannon. "Climb up!" he said.

"Wait," Shannon said. "I have to go back and help her!"

"Okay, but hurry!" Mike said.

Just then, smoke started to fill the warehouse.

"Enough games, children!" Mr. Bones's voice echoed off the metal walls.

The C. Yangi began to swoop down and head directly at them. "Shannon, come back!" Mike cried. "There's no time! We'll have to come back for her!"

At that point, Shannon couldn't see through the smoke. She let out a frustrated cry and turned back.

"We'll come back for you, Ms. Li Jing!" she said. "I swear it!"

Mr. Bones emerged from the smoke, gesturing with his right hand. "This isn't over!" growled Mr. Bones. "Give me that jacket, boy, or I'll have my other pet make you its next meal!"

The C. Yangi had nearly reached them. They could no longer see Ms. Li Jing in the smoke. They couldn't wait any longer. "Time's up," he said sadly.

"Do it!" Shannon cried, clambering up onto the dinosaur along with Mike and Ahfu. "But promise me we'll come back to get Ms. Li Jing!"

121

Mike nodded. "He hasn't seen the last of us," he said through clenched teeth.

Shannon wrapped her arms around Mike. He hit the button on the portal key

ZAP!!!

Mike, Shannon, Ahfu, and the P-Rex disappeared into the past.

GLOSSARY

Jurassic Period (juh-RASS-ik PEER-ee-uhd)—a period of time about 200 to 144 million years ago

fossil (ek-STINGKT)—the remains, impression, or trace of a living thing of a former geologic age, like a dinosaur bone

Changyuraptor Yangi (ek-STINGKT)—a four-winged predatory dinosaur, also known as C. Yangi

paleontologist (pale-ee-uhn-TOL-uh-jist)—a scientist who deals with fossils and other life-forms

Triceratops (try-SER-uh-tops)—a large, plant-eating dinosaur with three horns and a fan-shaped collar that is made of bone

Tyrannosaurus rex (ti-RAN-uh-sor-uhss)—a large, meat-eating dinosaur that walked on its hind legs, also known as a T. rex

DINO FACTS!

Lots of different kind of dinosaurs have roamed the Earth, but one of the weirdest ones was the Changyuraptor Yangi, a four-winged, meat-eating, high-flying dinosaur.

So far, paleontoligists have found only one fossil of the Changyuraptor Yangi, or C. Yangi for short. It was found in in the Liaoning Province, China, in 2014.

The bird-like dinosaur was about the length of a turkey. It likely lived in the Early Cretaceous period, an era between 100-140 million years ago.

C. Yangi is one of two dinosaur fossils that lead scientists to believe that the dinos had bird-like variations. The other fossil is the Microraptor, a raven-sized creature. It could fly and had long tail feathers.

Changyuraptor is a name made of Chinese and Latin words. The first part is Chinese, "cháng yǔ." It means "long feather." The second part of the name, raptor, is Latin for "robber."

The C. Yangi likely lived up to its name. It was a predatory dinosaur that would swoop down on its prey, or food, and grab them with its claws and mouth. Long-feathered robber, indeed!

ABOUT THE AUTHOR

Bronx, New York–born writer and artist Franco Aureliani has been drawing comics since he could hold a crayon. Currently residing in upstate New York with his wife, Ivette, and son, Nicolas, he spends most of his days in his Batcave-like studio where he works on comics projects. In 1995, Franco founded Blindwolf Studios, an independent art studio where he and fellow creators can create children's comics. Franco is the creator, artist, and writer of Weirdsville, L'il Creeps, and Eagle All Star, as well as the cocreator and writer of Patrick the Wolf Boy.

Franco recently finished work on Superman Family Adventures and Tiny Titans by DC Comics, and Itty Bitty Hellboy and Aw Yeah Comics by Dark Horse comics. When he's not writing and drawing, Franco teaches high school art.